ASTERIX AND THE BANQUET

TEXT BY GOSCINNY

DRAWINGS BY UDERZO

TRANSLATED BY ANTHEA BELL AND DEREK HOCKRIDGE

Hodder
Children's
Books

a division of Hodder Headline

British Library Cataloguing in Publication Data

Goscinny
  Asterix and the banquet. — (Knight books)
  I. Title   II. Uderzo, Albert
  741.5'944   PN6747

ISBN 0 340 32060 5

First published in Great Britain 1979 (cased) by Hodder Dargaud Ltd
This edition first published 1983 by Knight Books, Hodder Dargaud

13 12

Published by Hodder Children's Books, A division of Hodder Headline
338 Euston Road, London, NW1 3BH

Printed in Belgium by Proost International Book Production

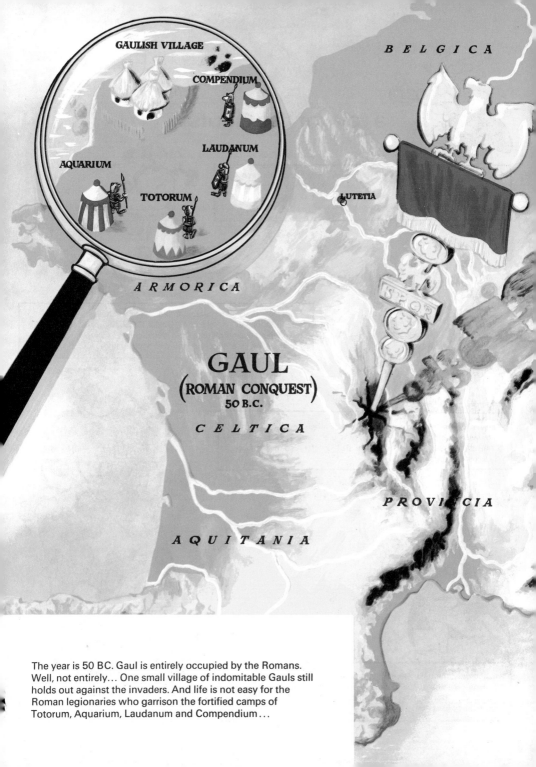

GAUL
(ROMAN CONQUEST)
50 B.C.

The year is 50 BC. Gaul is entirely occupied by the Romans. Well, not entirely… One small village of indomitable Gauls still holds out against the invaders. And life is not easy for the Roman legionaries who garrison the fortified camps of Totorum, Aquarium, Laudanum and Compendium…

a few of the Gauls

Asterix, the hero of these adventures. A shrewd, cunning little warrior; all perilous missions are immediately entrusted to him. Asterix gets his superhuman strength from the magic potion brewed by the druid Getafix...

Obelix, Asterix's inseparable friend. A menhir delivery-man by trade; addicted to wild boar. Obelix is always ready to drop everything and go off on a new adventure with Asterix — so long as there's wild boar to eat, and plenty of fighting.

Getafix, the venerable village druid. Gathers mistletoe and brews magic potions. His speciality is the potion which gives the drinker superhuman strength. But Getafix also has other recipes up his sleeve...

Cacofonix, the bard. Opinion is divided as to his musical gifts. Cacofonix thinks he's a genius. Everyone else thinks he's unspeakable. But so long as he doesn't speak, let alone sing, everybody likes him...

Finally, Vitalstatistix, the chief of the tribe. Majestic, brave and hot-tempered, the old warrior is respected by his men and feared by his enemies. Vitalstatistix himself has only one fear; he is afraid the sky may fall on his head tomorrow. But as he always says, 'Tomorrow never comes.'

PEACE REIGNS IN THE FORTIFIED ROMAN CAMP OF COMPENDIUM...

?!

♪♫

ZZZZ

UNTIL...

O CENTURION LOT-USEATUS, THERE'S A VISITOR FROM ROME FOR YOU. LOOKS LIKE TOP BRASS!

HE DOES?

AVE! I AM INSPECTOR GENERAL OVERANXIUS, WITH THE RANK OF PREFECT, ON A SPECIAL MISSION FROM JULIUS CAESAR!

AVE.

ER... PLEASED TO MEET YOU... AND HOW'S CAESAR?

FED TO THE TEETH, BY JUPITER! THAT'S WHY I'M HERE! ALL GAUL IS AT PEACE WITH THE LIBERATING ROMAN ARMY, EXCEPT THIS ONE LITTLE VILLAGE OF DISSIDENTS HERE IN YOUR SECTOR DEFYING THE POWER OF CAESAR!

S... SO?

SO I AM GOING TO LEAD YOUR MEN AGAINST THE VILLAGERS. I'LL SOON GET THEM INTO LINE!

BUT... BUT THOSE GAULS ARE DANGEROUS! THEY HAVE MAGICAL POWERS...

NONSENSE! SOUND THE ASSEMBLY!

WE'RE ENTERING THE LISTS! HOLD THE GAULS AT BAY, AND IT WILL BE ANOTHER BAYLEAF IN CAESAR'S WREATH! ✳

THE GAULS?!

✳ WE WOULD SAY: ANOTHER FEATHER IN HIS CAP.

DIRECTLY AFTERWARDS...

I DIDN'T MEAN THE SICK BAY! WHERE'S YOUR PILUM?

SICK BAY

IT MAY BE A BITTER PILUM, BUT WE PREFER THE SICK LISTS.

6

AND A SHORT, SHARP BATTLE BETWEEN GAULS AND ROMANS ENSUES...

PAF! PIF! BY JUPITER! TCHAC!

BY TOUTATIS! CHTAFF!

BYE-BYE! BING!

TCHRAAC!

I TELL YOU THIS ONE'S MINE, FULLIAUTOMATIX!

OH NO, IT ISN'T! OH NO, IT ISN'T! YOU'VE HAD FOUR ALREADY. I'VE BEEN COUNTING.

YOU CAN STOP ARGUING, THEY'RE OFF.

?!?

NO! NO! COME BACK! OH, PLEASE COME BACK!

IF WE'VE QUITE FINISHED, MAY I LEAVE THE BATTLEFIELD?

AND BACK IN COMPENDIUM...

SICK BAY

I ASK YOU! WAS IT WORTH BEING THUMPED JUST TO LAND UP BACK HERE?

I DID WARN YOU, OVERANXIUS!

GNGNGNGNGNGNGN GNGNGNGNGN!!

WELL, IF THAT'S HOW IT IS, I HAVE ANOTHER IDEA! WE SHALL ISOLATE THE GAULISH VILLAGE FROM THE OUTSIDE WORLD!

SOON AFTERWARDS...

EXEGI MONUMENTUM AERE PERENNIUS.

LET'S HOPE YOU'RE RIGHT!

CRAAC!

7

O CHIEF VITALSTATISTIX, THE ROMANS ARE PUTTING UP A STOCKADE ALL ROUND THE VILLAGE!

GOODNESS ME, WHAT FOR? LET'S TAKE A LOOK...

THESE ROMANS ARE CRAZY!

SINCE YOU'RE SO CLEVER, BY MINERVA, I'M SHUTTING YOU UP IN YOUR VILLAGE! YOU WON'T BE ABLE TO GO SPREADING YOUR SEDITIOUS OPINIONS THROUGH GAUL!

YOU'LL HAVE TO BE SELF-SUFFICIENT AND LIVE ON THE PRODUCE OF YOUR OWN VILLAGE! THE OUTSIDE WORLD WILL FORGET YOU!

GAUL IS OUR COUNTRY, O ROMAN, AND WE'LL GO WHERE WE LIKE IN IT...

I'LL MAKE A BET WITH YOU: WE SHALL GET OUT OF OUR VILLAGE IN SPITE OF YOUR STOCKADE AND YOUR LEGIONARIES, AND WE'LL GO ON A TOUR OF GAUL...

...BRINGING BACK ALL ITS REGIONAL SPECIALITIES! ON OUR RETURN, WE'LL INVITE YOU TO A BANQUET TO PROVE WE ARE TELLING THE TRUTH!

HARGH HARGH GNGNGNGH!!!

DONE, O GAULS! IF YOU WIN YOUR BET I WILL RAISE THE SIEGE AND GO BACK TO ROME TO TELL JULIUS CAESAR I'VE FAILED!

AND WHEN YOU GET THERE, GIVE OUR REGARDS TO OUR OLD FRIEND CAIUS FATUOUS.

KEEP AN EYE ON THEM!

AN EYE IT'LL HAVE TO BE... I CAN'T OPEN THE OTHER ONE YET!

8

THIS IS THE ROUTE WE'LL TAKE...

ASTERIX, HERE IS A GOURD OF MAGIC POTION TO SUSTAIN YOU ON YOUR LONG AND DANGEROUS JOURNEY.

THANKS, O GETAFIX!

SHALL I BRING A MENHIR, ASTERIX? YOU NEVER KNOW WHEN A MENHIR MAY COME IN HANDY.

NO, YOU'D BETTER BRING A BIG SHOPPING BAG TO HOLD ALL THE THINGS WE'LL BE BUYING FOR THE BANQUET ON OUR WAY THROUGH GAUL.

O CHIEF VITAL-STATISTIX, HOW ABOUT ATTACKING THE ROMANS AT THE SOUTH OF THE VILLAGE WHILE WE START OUT NORTH?

COUNT ON US, ASTERIX!

COME ON, OBELIX!

AFTER YOU, ASTERIX!

AND THIS IS THE START OF THE FAMOUS TOUR OF GAUL!

I WILL NOW SING A LITTLE...

OH NO, YOU WON'T! OH, NO YOU WON'T! OH NO, YOU WON'T!

RIGHT, LET'S GO AND ATTACK THE ROMANS AT THE SOUTH OF THE VILLAGE.

AFTER A FEW MOMENTS' FIGHTING...

STOP IT! STOP IT! STOP IT!

RIGHT, LET'S GO HOME TO THE VILLAGE. OUR FRIENDS WILL HAVE GOT A START, AND IT'S LATE.

PAF! BANG! BONG!

THERE'S A BREACH IN THE STOCKADE TO THE NORTH! THAT ATTACK WAS JUST A DIVERSION!

DIVERSION?!? I LIKE YOUR CHOICE OF WORDS!

WHILE THE GAULS WERE ATTACKING US TO THE SOUTH, SOME OF THEM GOT OUT HERE AFTER THUMPING THE SENTRY.

IF ONLY WE KNEW WHICH ONES!

JOIN THE ARMY, THEY SAID. IT'S A MAN'S LIFE, THEY SAID...

OH, THAT'S EASY! IT'LL HAVE BEEN ASTERIX AND OBELIX. THAT PAIR ARE ALWAYS TRYING TO MAKE US LOOK SILLY... AND REMEMBER, IT WAS ASTERIX WHO MADE THAT BET WITH YOU!

WELL, THEY WON'T GET FAR! I WANT THE ENTIRE ARMY OF OCCUPATION ALERTED ALL OVER GAUL! SEND A DESPATCH RIDER OFF AT ONCE!

WE'LL BE THE LAUGHING-STOCK OF GAUL IF THEY WIN THAT BET!

MEANWHILE...

WE MAY HAVE TIME TO REACH ROTOMAGUS* BEFORE THEY RAISE THE ALARM.

*ROUEN

AND FROM ROTOMAGUS WE CAN GO ALONG THE RIVER TO LUTETIA, OUR FIRST STOPPING PLACE.

LOOK, ASTERIX! THERE'S A ROMAN SOLDIER ON HORSE-BACK.

AFTER A LONG WALK...

O NORMAN FULFILLING YOUR NORM, IS THIS THE WAY TO ROTO-MAGUS?

COULD BE, COULDN'T SAY FOR SURE.

THOUGHT IT WAS A BUCKET HE WAS FILLING. IS IT FAR?

COULD BE, NOT, COULDN'T SAY FOR SURE.

THIS COULD BE IT, OBELIX, BUT I COULDN'T SAY FOR SURE...

ROTOMAGUS

10

YOU CAN STOP NOW, OBELIX. WE'VE GOT TO LUTETIA.

NOT TOO TIRED?

OH NO. CRUISING DOWN THE RIVER IS VERY RESTFUL.

THERE'S NOTHING TO WORRY ABOUT IN LUTETIA. THE ROMANS WILL NEVER FIND US IN THE CROWD

HULLO, THEY HAVEN'T SORTED IT OUT SINCE WE WERE LAST HERE.*

GET A MOVE ON!

YOU HEARD HIM! MOVE!

SO JUST WHERE DO I MOVE, GRANDPA?

I'VE BEEN HERE TWO DAYS NOW!

HEAR THAT? SOMEONE NEW!

* SEE ASTERIX AND THE GOLDEN SICKLE

THESE MINIS CAN NIP IN ANYWHERE!

WE'RE GOING TO BUY SOME HAM. LUTETIA IS FAMOUS FOR ITS HAM!

PORK BUTCHER

YES, A WHOLE HAM, AND DON'T SLICE IT TOO THIN...

GET YOUR CART OUT OF THE WAY! YOU'RE BLOCKING THE ROAD!

SO WHAT? I'M UNLOADING, AREN'T I?

WELL, HERE COMES A PATROL! WE'LL SEE WHAT THEY SAY ABOUT IT!

A PATROL! LET'S GET OUT!

13

*CAMBRAI...

17

WE'LL LEAVE THE CHARIOT HERE. IT'S A BIT TOO CONSPICUOUS.

WE MUSTN'T SPEND TOO LONG IN DUROCORTORUM. OUR PURSUERS CAN'T BE FAR BEHIND...

DO YOU SELL GOOD WINE?

YOU MUST BE JOKING! THE BEST WINE OF ALL! IT'S FIZZY AND SPARKLING. PEOPLE BUY IT FOR IMPORTANT OCCASIONS, LIKE LAUNCHING GALLEYS...

YOU WANT BRUT, SEC, DEMI-SEC, OR DOUX?

?!?   ?!?

WELL, TAKE AN AMPHORA OF EACH! WE KNOW ABOUT YOUR BET... BUT MUMM'S THE WORD!

THANK YOU VERY MUCH!

AND WATCH THE CORKS. THEY POP RATHER EASILY.

WINES

?!?

WE MEET AGAIN, GAULS! AND NOW I KNOW WHO YOU ARE! STAY PUT, OR YOU GET MY PILUM IN YOUR STERNUM!

PASS ME AN AMPHORA.

BRUT?

BRUT.

POP!   WHOOOSH!   PAF!

BRUTES!

WE MUST KEEP OFF THE ROADS, OBELIX... LET'S CUT THROUGH THE FOREST.

SOON AFTERWARDS.

I'M HUNGRY, ASTERIX... AND THERE'S SO MUCH TO EAT IN THE BAG...

WE MUSTN'T TOUCH IT, OBELIX. WE HAVE TO TAKE IT ALL HOME FOR THE BANQUET.

ASTERIX, I CAN SMELL ROAST BOAR!!!

SNIFF! SNIFF!

?!?

IT'S OVER THERE!

HE SEEMS TO THINK IT'S HEAVEN-SCENT...

SNIFF! SNIFF!

OBELIX, IT WOULD BE MORE SENSIBLE TO STICK TO A FEW ROOTS...

ROOTS ARE ALL RIGHT FOR BOARS, AND BOARS ARE ALL RIGHT FOR US, AND THAT WAY EVERYONE'S HAPPY, SO COME ON!

I'LL KNOCK!

NO, OBELIX! DON'T!

HOW MANY TIMES HAVE I TOLD YOU NOT TO GO KNOCKING AT DOORS?

SORRY, I FORGOT.

WHAT THE...

WHY, IT'S THOSE TWO GAULS THE ROMANS WANT... A LITTLE MAN AND A FAT MAN WITH A BAG!

MY FRIEND AND I WONDERED IF YOU COULD GIVE US A MEAL... OF COURSE WE'D PAY!

COME ALONG IN, BE MY GUESTS! I'M ALWAYS GLAD TO HELP A FELLOW GAUL, AS SURE AS MY NAME'S UNPATRIOTIX.

I'M AFRAID WE'RE IMPOSING...

I THINK I'M GOING TO IMPOSE A LITTLE MORE...

EAT UP, EAT UP! THE ROMANS WILL PAY HANDSOMELY FOR YOUR MEAL!

I COULD DO WITH A NAP AFTER SUCH A GOOD MEAL!

YES YOU SLEEP IT OFF! I'M JUST GOING OUT FOR A LITTLE WHILE...

AREN'T YOU HAVING A NAP, OBELIX?

NO, I'M GOING TO TAKE A LOOK AROUND AND SEE IF I CAN'T FIND ANOTHER BOAR. I'M STILL A BIT EMPTY...

MEANWHILE...

TREACHEROUS I MAY BE, BUT I'M NOT DOING THIS FOR NOTHING! I'M DOING IT FOR MONEY!

HALT, GAUL! WHAT DO YOU WANT?

TAKE ME TO YOUR LEADER! I HAVE IMPORTANT NEWS!

I'VE COME TO BETRAY THE TWO GAULS YOU'RE AFTER. THEY ARE IN MY HUT!

IF YOUR STORY'S TRUE, YOU GET 200 SESTERTII. IF NOT, YOU GET 200 LASHES.

HOW DARE YOU DOUBT MY WORD? A MAN'S WORD IS HIS BOND!

COME ON, MEN! THERE'S WORK TO BE DONE!

SOON AFTERWARDS...

THEY'RE IN THERE... ER... I THINK I'LL HIDE HERE, SO AS NOT TO GET IN YOUR WAY.

HOW VERY THOUGHTFUL OF YOU, UN-PATRIOTIX!

AND...

ONE MOVE AND YOU DIE, GAUL!!!

?!

I DIDN'T EVEN HAVE TIME TO TAKE A DROP OF MAGIC POTION!

HERE UN-PATRIOTIX, YOUR REWARD: 100 SESTERTII!

100 SESTERTII? BUT WE SAID 200!

200 FOR TWO GAULS. WE ONLY GOT ONE.

WH... WHAT? ONLY ONE??

BETTER GET OUT BEFORE THE OTHER ONE COMES BACK!

YOOHOO! ASTERIX! HERE I AM!

!!!

LOOK WHAT I FOUND, ASTERIX! I'LL LET YOU HAVE A LITTLE IF YOU LIKE.

HULLO, WHERE'S ASTERIX?

I... I DON'T KNOW... ER, YOUR FRIEND LEFT. I DIDN'T HAVE ANY REASON TO STOP HIM...

ASTERIX WOULD NEVER HAVE LEFT WITHOUT ME! WHERE IS HE?

MERCY! I'LL TALK!

I... I'M A MISFIT, YOU SEE, IT'S ALL BECAUSE OF MY UNDERPRIVILEGED ENVIRONMENTAL SITUATION, AND I BETRAYED ASTERIX TO THE ROMANS WHO TOOK HIM TO THE NEAREST GARRISON TOWN...

WHAT'S THIS TOWN CALLED?

DIVODURUM.

I DON'T CARE IF YOU'VE ORDERED RUM OR NOT. YOU DON'T SOFTEN ME UP LIKE THAT! WHERE'S ASTERIX?

IN DIVODURUM.✱ IT'S THE NAME OF TOWN. IT'S EAST OF HERE.

✱METZ...

I'LL NEVER BETRAY MY FELLOW-COUNTRY-MEN AGAIN. THE PAY'S GOOD, BUT IT'S DANGEROUS WORK...

...AND MORALLY INDEFENSIBLE.

HERE WE ARE... A GARRISON TOWN, HE SAID...

DIVODURUM

ASTERIX MUST HAVE BEEN TAKEN TO PRISON. NOW THE BEST WAY TO FIND THE PRISON AND GET INSIDE WOULD BE TO GET TAKEN TO PRISON MYSELF...

SO AS SOON AS I SEE A LEGIONARY I'LL SLAP HIS FACE AND HE'LL CART ME OFF TO PRISON... AH, HERE COMES A GOOD ONE!

PAF!

WELL, COME ON, THEN! PUT ME IN IRONS, CAN'T YOU? TAKE ME TO PRISON!

HEY, TAKE ME TO PRISON! I'VE KNOCKED OUT A LEGIONARY!

QUICK, LEAVE THE LEGIONARY THERE AND HIDE, OR THE ROMANS WILL TAKE YOU PRISONER!

BUT I WANT THEM TO TAKE ME PRISONER! I'M LOOKING FOR THE PRISON!

YOU ARE? WELL, IF YOU'RE SURE YOU WANT THE PRISON, TAKE THE THIRD TURNING ON THE RIGHT.

THANKS.

THIS IS YOURS. I KNOCKED HIM OUT. CAN I COME IN?

?!??

OBELIX!

ASTERIX! AT LAST! I'VE HAD TROUBLE FINDING YOU. COME ON, LET'S GO.

22

23

26

THEY'RE TRYING TO GET US LOST... LET'S RETRACE OUR STEPS!

AND SOON...

YOOHOO! ARE YOU THERE, FIBROSITUS?

NO, I'M HERE!

DON'T KNOW WHERE I AM!

JUST OUTSIDE THE MAZE...

THOSE WRETCHED GAULS ARE TRYING TO FOOL ME... I'M GOING IN TO LOOK FOR MY GARRISON!

BUT I SHALL LEAVE A TRAIL OF PEBBLES BEHIND ME, TO BE ON THE SAFE SIDE. ✳

✳ AN IDEA LATER TAKEN UP BY A FAMOUS TELLER OF FAIRY TALES, WHICH GOES TO SHOW THAT IMITATION IS THE SINCEREST FORM OF FLATTERY.

HEY, GARRISON, WHERE ARE YOU?

ON THE OTHER SIDE OF TOWN...

IT'LL TAKE THE ROMANS ALL DAY TO GET OUT... YOU CAN CARRY ON WITH YOUR JOURNEY. WE'VE GOT YOU A CHARIOT.

THE THING IS...

WE HAVE TO BUY SOMETHING FOR OUR BANQUET...THE LOCAL SPECIALITIES OF LUGDUNUM.

WE THOUGHT OF THAT. HERE: SAUSAGE AND MEAT-BALLS.

YOOHOO! ARE YOU THERE?

OH, WAS IT YOU WHO DROPPED ALL THOSE PEBBLES, O PREFECT POISONUS FUNGUS? HERE, I'VE BEEN PICKING THEM UP FOR YOU!

I WANT TO GET OUT OF HERE, DECURION!

NOW LET'S ALL KEEP CALM! DON'T PANIC!

HOW CAN WE THANK YOU?

BY WINNING YOUR BET, FRIENDS!

NOW, FULL SPEED AHEAD TO OUR NEXT PORT OF CALL, NICAE!*

CRACK!

*NICE

ROMAN ROAD VII, THAT'LL BE IT!

RR VII

?!?

GET A MOVE ON!

GET A MOVE ON WHERE, EH, GRANDPA?

IF I'D ONLY KNOWN...

IF IFS AND ANDS WERE CAULDRONS AND AMPHORAS...

WATCH OUT, YOU'LL RAM MY OXEN!

SERVICE STATION BH BEST HAY I MILIA PASSUM

WHAT'S GOING ON HERE?

DON'T YOU KNOW? THIS IS THE START OF THE SUMMER HOLIDAY, AND EVERYONE'S GOING SOUTH TO THE SEASIDE FOR PEACE AND QUIET!

GET OUT OF THAT CART IF YOU'RE A MAN!

I'VE BEEN IN THE ARMY, I HAVE! I'D HAVE YOU KNOW I FOUGHT WITH VERCINGETORIX AT GERGOVIA!

CALL THIS PEACE AND QUIET?

THESE LUTETIANS ARE CRAZY!

AN INN! LET'S STOP FOR A BITE AND A LITTLE REAL PEACE!

GOOD IDEA.

I ORDERED BOAR. THIS IS VEAL!

BOAR'S OFF, AND IF YOU DON'T WANT THAT VEAL THERE ARE PLENTY OF PEOPLE WAITING WHO DO!

FINALLY THE ROAD WINDS PAST OLIVE TREES...

THESE NORTHERNERS ARE CRAZY!

THAT DOES IT! HE GRAZED MY WING!

WELL, WHY DIDN'T YOU TAKE YOUR HELMET OFF THEN, GRANDPA?

HERE WE ARE, OBELIX! LET'S DUMP THE CHARIOT NOW.

NICAE

SO THIS IS THE GAULISH RIVIERA...

AND VERY NICE TOO... BUT COME ON, WE MUST BUY SOME OF THE LOCAL SPECIALITY.

AN AMPHORA OF SALAD TO TAKE AWAY, PLEASE.

IS SALAD FROM NICAE GOOD?

VERY GOOD! WELL, THAT WENT OFF ALL RIGHT. NEXT STOP MASSILIA.* LET'S GET GOING.

*MARSEILLES

LOOK! THAT'S THEM! A LITTLE MAN AND A BIG FAT MAN!

!?!

I AM NOT FAT! I AM NOT FAT! WELL-BUILT, MAYBE, NOT FAT!

DON'T LET'S STOP TO ARGUE, OBELIX.

STOP THOSE MEN!!

BIG FAT MAN! HONESTLY, I ASK YOU!

WATCH WHERE YOU'RE GOING!

SOME PEOPLE THINK THEY CAN TRAMPLE OVER EVERYONE!

IT'S ALL THESE PACKAGE TOURS!

OH, AND WHAT HAVE YOU GOT AGAINST PACKAGE TOURS?

GO CAREFULLY WITH THAT SHOPPING BAG. WE DON'T WANT TO GET IT WET.

IT'S LOVELY ONCE YOU'RE IN!

FOR JUPITER'S SAKE, STOP THEM!!!

THIS IS WHAT WE NEED!

NO! NO! I HIRED THIS BOAT FOR MYSELF! YOU'LL CAPSIZE IT!

WE'RE GOING OUT TO SEA! THIS IS MOST UNWISE! WHERE ARE YOU GOING?

MASSILIA.

FAT, INDEED! I'VE GOT A POWERFUL PHYSIQUE, THAT'S ALL.

BUT I DON'T WANT TO GO TO MASSILIA! I HAD A LOT OF TROUBLE FINDING A ROOM WITH FULL BOARD IN NICAE, AND I DON'T WANT TO MISS LUNCH!

WELL, THIS IS A BOARDING PARTY BOUND FOR MASSILIA, SO YOUR LUNCH WILL HAVE TO GO BY THE BOARD!

ANYWAY IT'S ALL MUSCLE. NOT AN OUNCE OF FAT, JUST MUSCLE!

At last, after a long sea journey, our friends tie up at the great port of Massilia...

THANKS FOR THE BOAT RIDE.

I THOUGHT IT WAS US TAKING HIM FOR A RIDE, ASTERIX?

HEY, YOU! WHERE ARE YOU TAKING THAT BOAT?

BACK TO NICAE. I'VE GOT A ROOM THERE, WITH FULL BOARD.

GOING BACK TO NICAE BY SEA? WHAT, WITH THE MISTRAL COMING UP? VESUVIUS ERUPTING IS NOTHING TO IT! ARE YOU CRAZY?

THIS IS THE LAST TIME I EVER GO TO THE SOUTH OF GAUL ON HOLIDAY!

TOUCH OF THE SUN, EH? THESE LUTETIANS ARE CRAZY!

DRINKLIKAFIX

TUNAFIX

LET'S GO IN FOR A BITE AND A SUP AND A LITTLE INFORMATION.

HEY, CÉSAR! COMPANY!

CAESAR?!

NO, NOT THAT ONE! I'M NOT JULIUS CAESAR, I'M CÉSAR DRINKLIKAFIX, LANDLORD OF THIS INN.

PLEASED TO MEET YOU... CAN YOU TELL US WHERE WE CAN BUY SOME FISH STEW TO TAKE AWAY?

FISH STEW?

HEY, HYDROPHOBIA! GET SOME FISH STEW COOKING!

HAVE A PASTIX?

NO THANKS, WE'D RATHER HAVE GOAT'S MILK...

AND A BOAR, IF YOU'VE GOT ONE...

GOAT'S MILK... BOAR... YOU WOULDN'T BE THE TWO GAULS THOSE CRAZY ROMANS ARE AFTER, WOULD YOU?

THAT'S US.

THEN WELCOME TO MASSILIA! DRINKS ALL ROUND ON ME! MILK FOR YOU, PASTIX FOR US!

NOT FOR ME, THANKS...

WHEN I OFFER DRINKS ON THE HOUSE, SIR, PEOPLE DRINK THEM, IF THEY DON'T WANT TO SEEM LIKE A FISH OUT OF WATER!

HURRY UP, OBELIX. I'D LIKE TO GET TO TOLOSA* AS SOON AS WE CAN.

IT'S NEARLY DARK...

*TOULOUSE

THERE YOU ARE, WHAT DID I SAY? CAN'T SEE A THING.

WELL, LET'S STOP HERE FOR THE NIGHT, OBELIX. WE CAN GO ON IN THE MORNING.

GOOD NIGHT, ASTERIX.

GOOD NIGHT, OBELIX.

ARE THOSE NEW RECRUITS?

NO! IT'S THE TWO GAULS!!

WE'VE SPENT THE NIGHT IN THE MIDDLE OF A ROMAN CAMP!

WHAT LUCK!

QUICK! GET THEM! WE'LL TAKE THEM TO PREFECT ADIPUS AT TOLOSA!

TANTANTARAA TARAA

?!!?

THERE ARE QUITE A LOT OF THEM. I'LL JUST TAKE A DROP OF MAGIC POTION...

MIND IF I START WITHOUT YOU, ASTERIX?

GET THEEEEEK!

PAF!

AND A FEW MINUTES AFTER THE TRUMPET HAS BLOWN REVEILLE...

I'VE BEEN THINKING, OBELIX... THAT ROMAN WANTED TO TAKE US TO TOLOSA. IT WOULDN'T BE A BAD IDEA TO LET THE ROMANS GIVE US TRANSPORT, WOULD IT?

NO... BUT WE'LL HAVE TO WAIT A BIT BEFORE WE CAN SUGGEST IT...

33

TH... THANKS.

DON'T MENTION IT.

THERE... THAT'S DONE.

RIGHT, NOW GO AND PUT MY FRIEND BACK IN CHAINS. WE'RE WASTING TIME!

DING! DING! DING!

STOP TREMBLING LIKE THAT, OR YOU'LL NEVER GET THE JOB DONE!

SNAP!

I'LL GIVE YOU A HAND, OR WE'LL BE HERE ALL DAY.

?!?

STOP IT, WILL YOU? STOP IT!!!

AND AT LAST...

THERE, CENTURION, THAT'S DONE. AVE.

JUST A MOMENT! WE FORGOT OUR SHOPPING BAG. IT'S OVER THERE!

SNAP!

DON'T WORRY, ASTERIX. I'LL GET IT.

SNAP!

BOOHOOHOO!

NOW, NOW, CALM DOWN. NEVER MIND. WE'LL PUT THEM IN THE CART WITHOUT CHAINING THEM UP.

SEB? THIS WAY WE'LL GET TO TOLOSA WITHOUT ANY TROUBLE. AND THE FUNNY THING IS WE'RE THE PRISONERS AND THEY'RE THE ONES TRUDGING ALONG ON FOOT!

THESE ROMANS ARE CRAZY!

AND AFTER A LONG, PEACEFUL JOURNEY...

WE'RE IN SIGHT OF TOLOSA. WAIT FOR ME HERE. I'M OFF TO TELL THE PREFECT WE'VE ARRIVED.

AFTER THIS GREAT VICTORY OF MINE I'M SURE TO GET AN ADMINISTRATIVE POST IN ROME.

TOLOSA

I WANT TO SEE THE PREFECT, AT ONCE! IT'S IMPORTANT.

WELL, CENTURION? YOU HAVE NEWS FOR ME?

YES, O PREFECT ADIPUS. I'D LIKE YOU TO COME TO THE OUTSKIRTS OF TOLOSA. I HAVE A LITTLE SURPRISE FOR YOU!

SOON AFTERWARDS.

I LIKE SURPRISES, AND THE EXERCISE WILL DO ME GOOD.

NEARLY THERE. THIS WILL BE QUITE A SURPRISE!

BY JUPITER!

THE PRISONERS! WHERE ARE THE PRISONERS?!

THIS IS YOUR SURPRISE? A SET OF SEMI-CONSCIOUS LEGIONARIES?

THEY WENT OFF SOON AFTER YOU LEFT... THEY SAID THEY HADN'T COME TO TOLOSA TO SEE ANY PREFECT, THEY WANTED SOME OF THE LOCAL SAUSAGE.

SAUSAGE? PREFECT? WHAT ON EARTH IS ALL THIS ABOUT, BY MINERVA?

NOTHING! NOTHING! FORGET IT!

SOBS

MEANWHILE OUR FRIENDS ARE LEAVING TOLOSA...

PRETTY PLACE, TOLOSA... IS THE SAUSAGE NICE?

SNIF SNIF

DELICIOUS, OBELIX!

ALL OVER GAUL, THE INFURIATED ROMANS ARE PUTTING UP POSTERS OFFERING A REWARD FOR THE CAPTURE OF OUR FRIENDS...

50,000 SESTERTII REWARD FOR INFORMATION LEADING TO THE ARREST OF

ASTERIX & OBELIX THE TWO DANGEROUS OUTLAWS

AND IN THE TOWN OF AGINUM...

GOOD FOR THEM!

YOU COULDN'T CALL THEM HANDSOME, BUT THEY HAVE CHARISMA!

I WONDER IF THEY'LL BE STOPPING HERE ON THEIR TOUR OF GAUL?

I'M SURE THEY WILL. THEY'LL WANT TO BUY OUR FAMOUS PRUNES. I HEARD THEY'VE BEEN SEEN IN TOLOSA!

50,000 SESTERTII REWARD FOR INFORMATION LEADING TO THE ARREST OF

ASTERIX & OBELIX THE TWO DANGEROUS OUTLAWS

IN THE ROMAN GARRISON COMMANDER'S OFFICE...

THESE TWO GAULS ARE VERY STRONG. I'VE THOUGHT OF A CUNNING STRATAGEM...

I'LL GIVE THEM DRUGGED FOOD TO EAT, THEY WILL FALL ASLEEP, AND ALL YOU HAVE TO DO IS PICK THEM UP FROM MY INN.

NOT THE KIND OF THING I REALLY LIKE, BUT ALL RIGHT, UPTOTRIX.

NOT A MOMENT TO LOSE! I MUST GO AND MEET THEM!

THEY'RE COMING! THEY'RE COMING!

ASTERIX AND OBELIX'S TOUR OF GAUL IS MORE LIKE A ROMAN TRIUMPH...

THREE CHEERS!

VERY NICE OF THEM, BUT THE ROMANS MIGHT NOTICE SOMETHING...

KEEP GOING!

WAIT A MINUTE, FRIENDS! YOU ARE NATIONAL HEROES...WOULD YOU DO ME THE HONOUR OF TAKING REFRESHMENT AT MY HUMBLE INN?

?!?...

MY NAME IS UPTOTRIX. I CAN OFFER YOU PRUNES AND WILD BOAR!

LET'S BE CAREFUL, OBELIX. WE'VE ALREADY BEEN BETRAYED ONCE.

BOAR! OH, COME ON ASTERIX!

MUST BE NICE TO BE ABLE TO DROP OFF SO EASILY!

LET'S GET OUT OF HERE. THE ROMANS CAN WAKE UP MINE HOST!

WE CAN MOVE MORE FREELY WITHOUT THE CART... BUT YOU'D BETTER GIVE ME THE BAG. THE POOR HORSE CAN'T CARRY ITS WEIGHT AS WELL AS YOURS.

MY WEIGHT? WHAT ABOUT MY WEIGHT?

IT'S TOO HEAVY, THAT'S WHAT ABOUT YOUR WEIGHT! HAND ME THAT BAG AND DON'T BE SO PIG-HEADED!

OH YES, MISTER ASTERIX ALWAYS GIVES THE ORDERS! MISTER ASTERIX IS THE BOSS! MISTER ASTERIX IS ALWAYS RIGHT!

WELL, IF THE HORSE CAN'T CARRY ME AND THE BAG, THEN WE'LL CARRY THE HORSE.

PROLONGED SULKS

THERE, WHAT DID I SAY?

?

PLOF!

OOF!

NO SUCH THING! THAT WAS A LONG LAP AND HE'S TIRED, THAT'S ALL!

YOU KNOW THAT WASN'T IT, OBELIX, BUT YOU'RE RIGHT, IT WAS A LONG LAP. LET'S STOP HERE FOR SOME SLEEP.

IN THE NIGHT...

TRAVELLERS! LET'S STEAL THEIR LUGGAGE!

YEAH!

RRRR RRRR

ZZZZ

PSST! WAKE-UP! COCK-A-DOODLE-DO! COCK-A-DOODLE-DO!

WHAT?

COME ON, OBELIX. TIME TO GET UP!

COCK-A-DOODLE-DO!

JUST A FEW MORE MINUTES!

RIGHT, MY HORSE IS RESTED NOW. WHERE DID YOU PUT THE BAG, ASTERIX?

THE BAG? I NEVER TOUCHED THE BAG!!!

BUT I LEFT IT HERE!

LET'S FACE IT, OBELIX, SOMEONE HAS STOLEN OUR SHOPPING!

OBELIX, WE MUST FIND IT! WITHOUT THAT BAG WE'LL HAVE FAILED! IT'S HEAVY, SO THE THIEVES CAN'T HAVE GOT FAR WITH IT. LET'S GO!

GEE UP!

HIM AGAIN? WHY AM I ALWAYS SADDLED WITH HIM?

GOT YOU NOW, GAULS!

QUICK, OBELIX, LET'S HIDE!

BUT I TELL YOU WE AREN'T ASTERIX AND OBELIX! WE MAY BE HIGHWAYMEN, BUT WE'RE ROMAN HIGHWAYMEN. OUR NAMES ARE VILLANUS AND UNSCRUPULUS.

DON'T MAKE ME LAUGH, BY SATURN! YOU FIT THE DESCRIPTION: A LITTLE MAN AND A BIG FAT MAN CARRYING A BAG.

I'LL TEACH YOU TO CARRY ON ABOUT BIG FAT MEN!

CALM DOWN, OBELIX! LET'S FOLLOW THEM AT A DISTANCE.

NEWS OF THE SENSATIONAL CAPTURE HAS REACHED THE TOWN OF BURDIGALA*.

WHAT A SHAME!

OUR POOR FELLOW-COUNTRYMEN!

TO FAIL AT THIS STAGE!

IF ONLY WE COULD HELP THEM!

* BORDEAUX

ASTERIX & OBELIX, THE TWO GAULS WHO DARED DEFY ROME, WILL BE PUT ON SHOW IN THE MAIN SQUARE OF BURDIGALA AS AN EXAMPLE TO OTHERS. GENERAL MOTUS WILL GIVE AN ADDRESS.

...AND THIS BAG OF FOOD, DESTINED FOR THE GAULISH BANQUET, IS PROOF POSITIVE THAT THESE TWO NOTORIOUS OUTLAWS, WHO DARED DEFY THE MIGHT OF ROME, HAVE FAILED IN THEIR ATTEMPT!

BUT I TELL YOU WE'RE VILLANUS...

...AND UNSCRUPULUS!

THEY'RE TELLING THE TRUTH!

?!

AND WE'D LIKE OUR SHOPPING BAG BACK. WE'RE IN A HURRY.

ASTÉRIX AND OBÉLIX! THREE CHEERS! COME ON, LADS, HELP THEM! OUR HEROES!

LEGIONARIES! SEIZE THOSE MEN!

41

THEY'RE ALL JOINING IN TO HELP US! GET THE SHOPPING BAG, OBELIX!

BAG, EH? LEGIONARIES, BAG THOSE MEN! CAESAR NEEDS THEM FOR HIS DIPLOMATIC POLICIES! GO ON, BAG THEM! *

TCHAC!

BANG!

* HENCE THE EXPRESSION: A DIPLOMATIC BAG

I'VE GOT THE BAG, ASTERIX. SHALL WE STAY TO JOIN THE FUN?

NO, THEY'RE DOING NICELY WITHOUT US, AND WE'RE IN A HURRY.

'SCUSE ME.

'SCUSE ME.

'SCUSE ME.

WAIT A MINUTE! WE WANT SOME OF THE LOCAL SPECIALITIES.

WE'D LIKE AN AMPHORA OF WHITE BURDIGALA, AND SOME OYSTERS TO TAKE AWAY, PLEASE.

WHAT'S UP IN TOWN?

SPECIALITIES OF BURDIGALA

BURDIGALA WINE

OH, I DON'T KNOW... SOME KIND OF RIOT.

OYSTERS ARE ALL RIGHT, BUT YOU CAN EAT BOAR EVEN WHEN THERE ISN'T AN R IN THE MONTH...

WHITE BURDIGALA

HOWEVER, THE RIOT IS OVER...

WELL, NOW DO YOU BELIEVE WE AREN'T GAULS? TOOK A BATTLE TO CONVINCE YOU, EH?

RELEASE THOSE MEN...

AND DON'T TALK TO ME ABOUT BATTLES ANY MORE! DON'T TALK TO ME ABOUT GAULS ANY MORE! DON'T TALK TO ME ABOUT ANYTHING ANY MORE!!!

LET'S MAKE FOR THE HARBOUR. WE'LL SEE IF WE CAN BOARD A SHIP FOR HOME...

HURRY UP UNLOADING, YOU LAZY LOT, OR I'LL MISS THE TIDE!

MENHIRS!

YOU'RE FROM ARMORICA?

YES, CAPTAIN SENIORSERVIX, FROM GESOCRIBATUM.* I'M GOING BACK TO ARMORICA AS SOON AS MY CARGO'S UNLOADED.

* LE CONQUET

CAN WE COME WITH YOU?

I'LL SEE TO YOUR MENHIRS. I KNOW HOW TO HANDLE MENHIRS!

SEE?

?!?

AND SOON

I THINK THAT'S THE LOT!

WHY, YOU MUST BE ASTERIX AND OBELIX! IT WILL BE AN HONOUR TO HAVE YOU ON BOARD MY SHIP!

THANK YOU, CAPTAIN!

AND...

CAST OFF THERE!

HEY! THERE SHOULD BE 39 ARTICLES! I'M STILL 4 SHORT. YOU'VE GOT MY ORDERS WRONG!

SORRY... ANOTHER MENHIR COMING OVER. CATCH!

BOF!

... STILL 3 SHORT, AND I'M FORESHORTENED! THIS GAME'S NOT WORTH THE CANDLE!

THERE'S NO DANGER OF MEETING ANY ROMANS. THEIR GALLEYS DON'T VENTURE THIS FAR... BUT THERE ARE PIRATES ABOUT!

YOU REALLY THINK WE MIGHT MEET PIRATES?

SURE ENOUGH, ON BOARD ANOTHER SHIP...

AFTER OUR LAST FIGHT, ERIX, WE HAD TO DO AN HONEST JOB OF WORK AND SAVE UP FOR A NEW BOAT... WE HAVEN'T FINISHED PAYING OFF THE INSTALMENTS YET, SO HERE'S HOPING FOR A VICTIM!

VICTIM TO STARBOARD!

PIRATE TO PORT!

GOODY!

RIGHT, LADS, NOW TAKE IT EASY. DON'T DO ANYTHING RASH! WE MUSTN'T FAIL THIS TIME!

WHY... IT'S...
IT'S THEM AGAIN!

GO ABOUT! QUICK, QUICK! GO ABOUT!

BUT TOO LATE...

VICTRIX CAUSA DIIS PLACUIT, SED VICTA CATONI.

I DON'T GO OVERBOARD FOR YOUR SENSE OF HUMOUR. YOU'D BETTER GO ABOUT LOOKING FOR A NEW JOB!

JUST COMING IN TO GESOSCRIBATUM, FRIENDS. IT'S A MILITARY PORT, SO IT'S FULL OF ROMAN GALLEYS AND LEGIONARIES ...WE MUST GET YOU ON LAND IN DISGUISE...

I KNOW! WE'LL LAND YOU HIDDEN IN SACKS.

WELL, ALL RIGHT. WE DON'T WANT TO MAKE TROUBLE FOR YOU.

SOON AFTER THE SHIP HAS TIED UP AT GESOCRIBATUM ...

PHEW! HE ISN'T HALF FAT!

WHO...IS... FAT?

SSH! IT'S ME, I'M FAT. SSH!

WHAT WAS THAT?

I... I WAS JUST SAYING I'M FAT.

??

CRAZY! QUITE CRAZY!

DON'T WORRY, YOU'RE NOT FAT!

GOOD!

DON'T COME OUT YET! THERE ARE TOO MANY ROMANS ABOUT. I'LL TELL YOU WHEN THE COAST'S CLEAR.

ALL RIGHT, BUT DID YOU KNOW YOU'RE TALKING TO OUR SHOPPING BAG?

PATROL HALT! NUMBER OFF ONE TO FOUR!

I II III IV

WELL, OUR TOUR OF GAUL IS NEARLY OVER, OBELIX.

YES, WE'RE NOT FAR FROM HOME NOW, ASTERIX!

LOOK...THE STOCKADE ROUND OUR VILLAGE...

WAIT A MINUTE. I'LL JUST FINISH OFF THE MAGIC POTION...

AND NOW LET'S GET THEM, OBELIX!!!

YOU SHALL NOT PASS!

WANT ME TO HOLD THE BAG, OBELIX?

BOOM! PAF! PIF! CLANG! BAM!

NO THANKS, OBELIX. I CAN MANAGE NICELY WITH ONE HAND.

I THINK WE CAN PASS NOW, ASTERIX. WE'VE GONE THROUGH THE FORMALITIES.

HOLD ON. I MUST WAKE ONE OF THEM UP.

STOP HITTING ME!

PAF! PAF! PAF!

GO AND TELL INSPECTOR GENERAL OVERANXIUS WE'RE BACK FROM OUR TOUR OF GAUL, AND WE INVITE HIM TO A BANQUET TO PROVE WE'VE WON OUR BET. IT'S IN THE BAG!

AT LAST...

JUST A LITTLE SONG OF WELCOME...

NO!

AND THAT EVENING OVER-ANXIUS COMES, GNASHING HIS TEETH, TO SINK THEM IN THE EVIDENCE...

HERE ARE THE THINGS TO EAT AND DRINK WE'VE BROUGHT BACK FROM ALL OVER GAUL... HAM FROM LUTETIA, HUMBUGS FROM CAMARACUM, DUROCORTORUM WINE...

...SAUSAGE FROM TOLOSA, SAUSAGE FROM LUGDUNUM, SALAD FROM NICAE, FISH STEW FROM MASSILIA, OYSTERS AND WINE FROM BURDIGALA.

BUT THERE'S STILL ONE COURSE MISSING... THE SPECIALITY OF THIS VILLAGE!

QUITE RIGHT, OBELIX!

WOOF! WOOF!

?!

O, OVERANXIUS. YOU KNOW WHICH CUT OF MEAT IS OUR OWN SPECIALITY?

?

THE UPPERCUT!

TCHAC!

AND OUR FRIENDS HOLD A MAGNIFICENT BANQUET TO CELEBRATE THEIR TRIUMPHANT TOUR OF GAUL, PUTTING BACK ALL THE DELICIOUS FOOD AND WINE OF THEIR BEAUTIFUL AND BELOVED COUNTRY... AS INSPECTOR GENERAL OVERANXIUS COULD CONFIRM, IT IS A GENUINE THREE-STAR MEAL...

THE END